The Boy Who Wouldn't Speak

by Steve Berry
art by Deirdre Betteridge

Annick Press Ltd.
Toronto • New York

Third printing, March 1998

Annick Press Ltd.

We acknowledge the support of the Canada Council
for the Arts for our publishing program.
We also thank the Ontario Arts Council.

THE CANADA COUNCIL | LE CONSEIL DES ARTS
FOR THE ARTS | DU CANADA
SINCE 1957 | DEPUIS 1957

Cataloguing in Publication Data
Berry, Steve, 1951 -
   The boy who wouldn't speak

ISBN 1-55037-231-9 (lib.)
ISBN 1-55037-230-0 (pbk.)

PS8553.E77B6 1992 jC813'.54 C91-095752-5
PZ7.B47Bo 1992

The art in this book was rendered in watercolour.
The text was typeset in Century Oldstyle by Attic Typesetting.

Distributed in Canada by:
Firefly Books Ltd.
3680 Victoria Park Avenue
Willowdale, ON
M2H 3K1

Published in the U.S.A. by Annick Press (U.S.) Ltd.
Distributed in the U.S.A. by:
Firefly Books (U.S.) Inc.
P.O. Box 1338
Ellicott Station
Buffalo, NY 14205

Printed and bound in Canada by
Friesens, Altona, Manitoba.

S.B. — To Ann and the boys

D.B. — For Adam

Owen was a boy who never spoke. Never. Not a word. His dad would say, "Hi there Owen, how are you today?" But Owen would just nod and smile.

His mom would say, "Who's my beautiful boy?" Owen would wave and smile happily.

When his brother Dylan asked, "Owen, would you like to climb the apple tree in the backyard?" Owen would laugh and smile and smile. But he wouldn't talk. Not a word.

His dad said to his mom, "I think there's something wrong with that boy. He doesn't talk. He won't even say his own name."

Owen's mom said, "No way. There's nothing wrong with him. He'll talk as soon as he's ready."

"But he's three years old!" said his dad. "Shouldn't he be ready now? Owen, say something to daddy...please!" But Owen just sat there and clapped his hands and rolled around on the floor laughing to himself.

By Owen's fifth birthday, his father was really worried. "That boy still won't say anything, not even his own name. We must take him to the doctor," he said.

"Nope," his mom said. "He'll talk when he's ready, won't you Owen?"

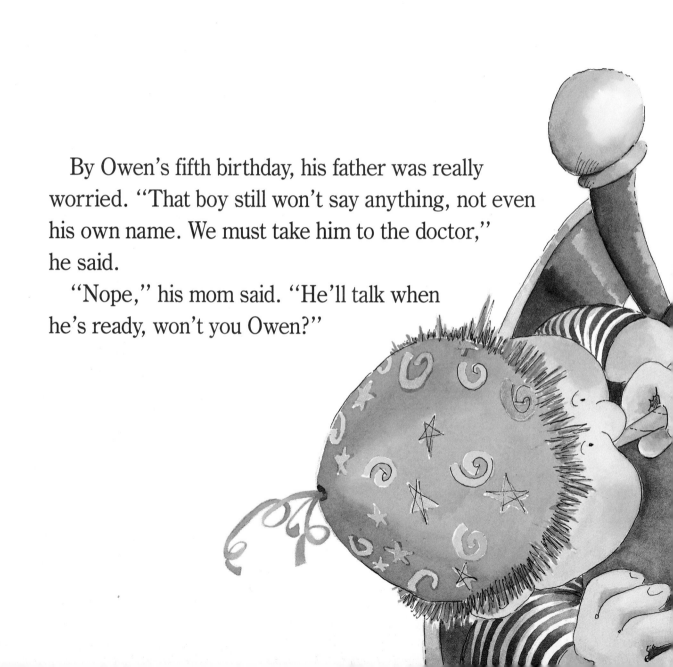

But it was time for Owen's check-up, so off they went to the doctor. The doctor said, "Hi, Owen. How are you today?" Owen gave her a big thumbs up sign.

"Still not saying anything, huh? Let's have a look."

She looked down Owen's throat and said, "Say AHHHHH." But Owen didn't. Then she said, "cough." Owen did. She gave him the rest of his check-up and then tickled him. Owen laughed.

The doctor smiled at Owen's mom. "There's nothing wrong with him that I can see. He'll talk when he's ready."

Owen smiled and nodded.

The next day Owen and Dylan were playing with their trucks when they heard a huge noise. They looked up and saw a SUPER-LARGE moving van. Two SUPER-LARGE GIANTS were moving into the house at the end of the block.

The man giant was dressed in the biggest pair of overall jeans Owen had ever seen. The lady giant wore a red track suit that was ENORMOUS! And her sandals made a big SMACK every time she took a step.

Dylan said, "Let's get out of here!" And he ran home to tell his mom what was going on. But Owen stood there smiling at the giants for a minute. And they smiled back. Then, with a wave goodbye, they went into their house.

When Owen got home, Dylan was telling his mother about the giants. "That's nice dear," she said, still trying to figure out some numbers at her desk.

"Owen," Dylan whined, "you tell her."

But Owen was already
on his way back to visit the giants.

He knocked on the door. The man giant
opened it and said, "Hi there, what's your name?" Owen
just smiled. "Cat got your tongue, eh? Well, come in and
play a while. My name is Fred and this is my wife, Lola."

The giants taught
Owen a card game
called "Giant's Bluff." They told him stories
about the land of giants. "Everyone there is big
like us, but we thought we'd come here and see if
we liked it," said Fred.

"If everyone is as friendly as you," said Lola,
"I'm sure we will."

They didn't seem to care that Owen didn't
talk. Owen visited Fred and Lola everyday.
The giants were always glad to see him.
They gave him milk and cookies and told
him more stories about their old home.
Sometimes they would make popcorn
and play games or watch television.
Once in a while Lola would make
some of her special baked ice
cream that was hot on the outside
and cold on the inside.

Best of all, the giants loved to dance. They would put on some music and do a slow waltz together. It looked so pretty and sometimes they would pick him up and he would dance with them. It was better than a ride in dad's car!

They were Owen's best friends.

But after a while Owen noticed that Fred and Lola were getting a little sad and they didn't waltz any more.

"We can't understand why no one has come to say hello to us," said Lola softly.

"Maybe they don't like giants," said Fred sadly.

And that's what was happening. People on Owen's block were afraid of them because they were so big, and they had all read stories about the terrible things that giants do.

"We can't have giants living on the block," said one lady. "You know what that means. Pretty soon there will be nothing but giants living here and there'll be no room for the rest of us."

A man who lived just two houses away from Owen said he wouldn't let his kids go anywhere near the giant's house, because he had heard that they eat little children! But Owen knew the man didn't even have kids. And he knew that Fred and Lola ate cookies and popcorn and baked ice cream, not kids.

The next time Owen went to visit the giants he discovered that the people on the street had sent a letter to the giants telling them they had to move away.

Fred and Lola got mad. "They can't tell us what to do," said Fred.

"You tell them Fred!" exclaimed Lola as she huffed and puffed and swelled up.

One day as Owen was walking home, he saw some of the neighbours marching towards Fred and Lola's house. They looked madder than mad. They were shouting about how they didn't want any giants living on their block.

"GO HOME GIANTS!" they yelled. "GO HOME GIANTS!"

Fred and Lola came out and stood on their front porch.

Owen stood right in the middle of them all. The yelling got louder and louder. Things had become VERY SCARY.

Suddenly,
somebody yelled,
"QUIETTTTTT!"
Everyone stopped shouting. They
looked at each other; then they looked at
Owen.

"QUIETTTTTT!" shouted Owen, again.
Everyone was shocked. Owen, the boy who
wouldn't speak, was talking.

"Listen," he said, "these guys, the giants, are my friends. Their names are Fred and Lola and they love to dance the waltz. And Lola knows how to bake ice cream. They tell me stories about their old home and they help me with my homework. They're only mad because nobody came to say hello and then everybody tried to throw them off our block, without even knowing anything about them. They're just like everyone else, but bigger."

All the neighbours stayed silent for a minute, just staring at Owen. Then they looked way up at Fred and Lola, who were looking at him too with nice, caring smiles on their faces. Nobody was really sure what to say.

Then the lady who had written the letter spoke, "They like to dance?" she asked nervously. "Why, I love to dance. Maybe they can teach me to waltz and I'll teach them how to do the two-step."

"Yeah, and maybe I'll teach them how to cook roast beef and Lola can teach me how to bake ice cream," said the man who thought giants only ate children.

Everyone was talking at once. The neighbours were smiling. Fred and Lola were smiling. Everyone was having a great time. Lola brought out some cookies and the whole neighborhood had a party right there on the street.

Owen's dad put his hand on Owen's shoulder. "That was a wonderful thing you did, son. I'm very proud of you."

"Thanks Dad," said Owen, smiling.

"There's just one thing I want to know," said his dad. "How come you waited until now to say something?"

"Because I didn't have anything important to say before now!" said Owen, laughing, as he ran back to get another of Lola's cookies.